D A N   Y A C C A R I N O

DOUG UNPLUGGED

ALFRED A. KNOPF   NEW YORK

This is Doug. He's a robot.

Each morning his parents plug him in to fill him up with lots and lots of facts. They love their little robot and want him to be the smartest robot ever.

"Today you will be learning all about the city," said his mom.

"Happy downloading," said his dad.

Doug learned about many city things:

Population: There are 8,175,133.5 people living in the city. . . .

Trash cans: People in the city throw out over 14,000 tons of trash each day. . . .

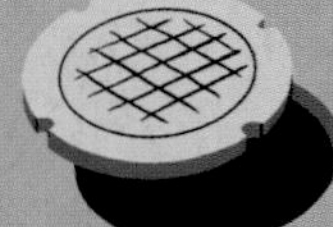

Manholes: There are 750,000 manholes. . . .

Fountains: The city's fountains pump 100 gallons of water every minute. . . .

Fire engines: Firefighters respond to more than 195 calls each day. . . .

Subways: There are 840 miles of subway tracks and 468 stations. . . .

Skyscrapers: The tallest skyscraper in the city has 102 floors. . . .

Fire hydrants: The first fire hydrant was installed in the city in 1808. . . .

Taxis: There are 13,237 yellow cabs making more than 470,000 trips each day. . . .

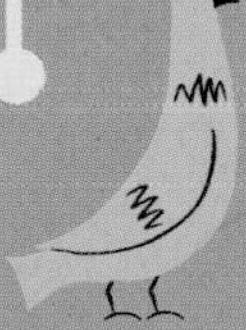

Pigeons: More than 500 million pigeons live in the city. . . .

But then something caught his eye.

It was a pigeon!

Doug had just learned that pigeons traveled in groups called flocks, but he didn't know they made such a funny cooing sound!

He wondered if there were more things he could learn if he went out into the city. So . . .

Doug unplugged!

Right away he learned that if you flew into a flock of pigeons, they scattered!

Doug knew that cities were teeming with people.

But he discovered that crowded sidewalks made it hard to see where you were going.

Doug found the subway! He already knew that subway trains ran underneath the entire city.

And that kids rode for free.

And now he found out that subway trains
s-c-r-e-e-e-e-c-h-e-d their way around corners.

He couldn't wait to learn more!

Doug knew that skyscrapers had strong steel frames so they could be many stories high.

But he was amazed by the view from the top of one! He could see everything!

Doug learned many more things about the city, like:

Wet cement feels squishy under your feet.

Fire engine sirens are loud.

Some garbage cans are smelly.

Manholes are dark.

Pretty flowers grow out
of cracks in the sidewalk.

Taxis stop if you raise your hand.

And the cool water in a park fountain feels good on a hot day.

Then Doug came across something that wasn't in any of his downloads.

"Want to play?" asked a little boy. Doug didn't know anything about playing, but he was happy to learn.

Doug learned how to play hide-and-seek.

And a new game called tag.

Doug found out there were all sorts of different ways to play.

And that it was nice to have a friend to play with.

“I don’t see my mom or dad!” his friend said, sounding scared. Doug remembered a way to get a better view of things.

So . . .

ZOOM!

They flew way up high.
“There they are!” the little boy shouted.

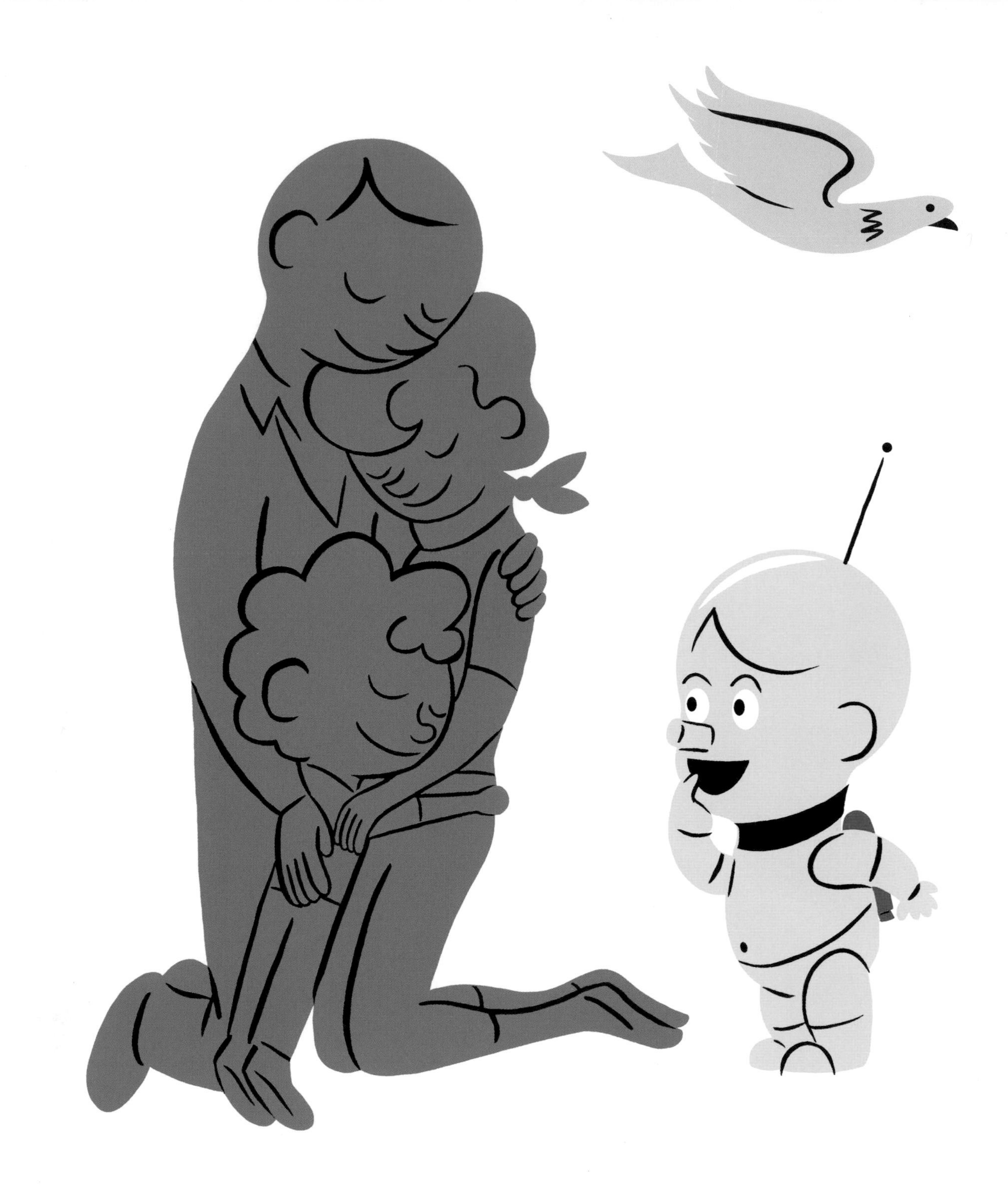

When they landed, the little boy ran to his mother and father. Doug thought about his own parents.

Suddenly he wanted to tell them everything he had learned today.

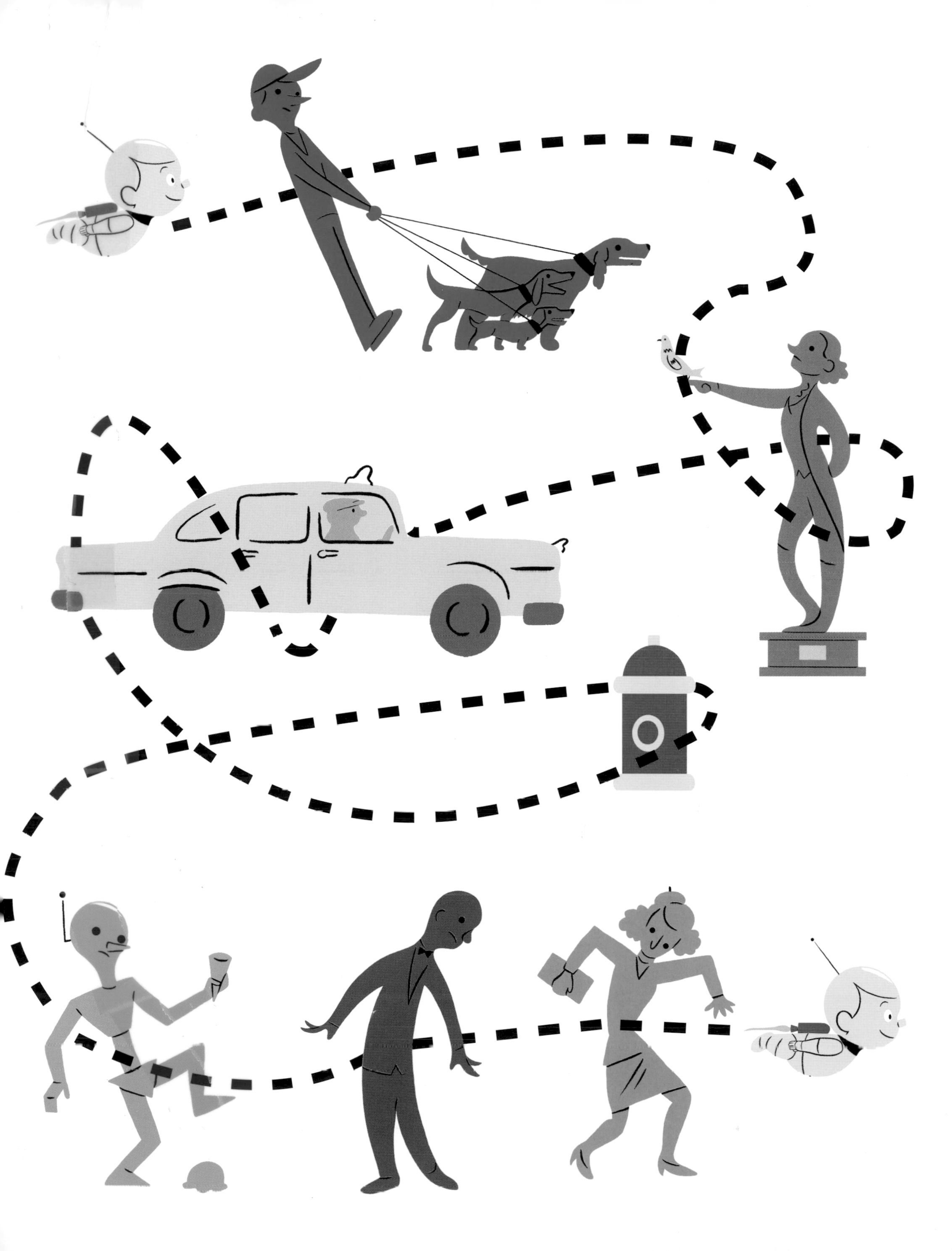

The best thing he learned was that if you want to show your parents you love them, you should give them a great big hug. And his parents thought he was the smartest robot ever.

For Will

THIS IS A BORZOI BOOK PUBLISHED BY ALFRED A. KNOPF

 Published in the United States by Alfred A. Knopf,
an imprint of Random House Children's Books, a division of Random House, Inc., New York.
Knopf, Borzoi Books, and the colophon are registered trademarks of Random House, Inc.
Visit us on the Web! randomhouse.com/kids
Educators and librarians, for a variety of teaching tools,
visit us at RHTeachersLibrarians.com

Library of Congress Cataloging-in-Publication Data
Yaccarino, Dan.
Doug unplugged / Dan Yaccarino. — 1st ed.
p. cm.
Summary: Doug the robot discovers that cities are much more than downloaded facts when he unplugs from the computer feed and explores one first-hand.
ISBN 978-0-375-86643-2 (trade) — ISBN 978-0-375-96643-9 (lib. bdg.)
[1. Robots—Fiction. 2. City and town life—Fiction.] I. Title.
PZ7.Y125Do 2013
[E]—dc23
2011047496

The illustrations in this book were created with brush and ink on vellum and Photoshop.

MANUFACTURED IN MALAYSIA
February 2013 10 9 8 7 6 5 4 3 2 1 First Edition